Trucks

Angela Royston

Illustrated by
Chris Forsey

Heinemann Interactive Library
Des Plaines, Illinois

Contents

© 1998 Reed Educational & Professional Publishing
Published by Heinemann Interactive Library, an imprint of Reed Educational & Professional Publishing,
1350 East Touhy Avenue, Suite 240 West
Des Plaines, Illinois 60018

Library of Congress Cataloging-in-Publication Data
Royston, Angela.
    Trucks / Angela Royston; illustrated by Chris Forsey.
        p. cm. — (Inside and out)
    Includes bibliographical references and index.
    Summary: Captioned illustrations and photographs along
with text identify types of trucks and their uses.
        ISBN 1-57572-181-3
        1. Trucks — Juvenile literature [1. Trucks.] I. Forsey, Christopher, ill.
II. Title. III. Series: Royston, Angela. Inside and out.
TL230.15.R68   1997   97-19337
629.224 — dc21   CIP
                                                                        AC

Photo credits: page 4 (top right): Trip © F Good; page 4 (bottom left): Environmental Images © Alex Olah;
page 6: © Brinks Security; page 9: © ZEFA-DAMM; page 10: © LAT Photographic; page 15: © ZEFA; page 17: Trip © M Lee;
page 18: © ZEFA; page 19: ZEFA © K Kummels; page 22: Panos Pictures © Liba Taylor.

Editor: Alyson Jones; Designer: Peter Clayman; Picture Researcher: Liz Eddison
Art Director: Cathy Tincknell; Production Controller: Lorraine Stebbing

Printed and bound in Italy.
See-through pages printed by SMIC, France.

02 01 00 99 98
10 9 8 7 6 5 4 3 2 1

Carrying Goods

Trucks carry things from one place to another. Some trucks are like huge boxes on wheels. They can carry almost anything. Can you tell what these trucks are carrying?

The part of the truck where the driver sits is called the cab. This driver from Pakistan has decorated his cab with colorful pictures.

Look at this truck packed with people and many different things. Can you see what is inside the sacks tied to the roof?

Special Trucks

Some trucks are built to do one job. This cement mixer brings ready-mixed cement to the building site. The large drum turns round and round to keep the cement soft and runny. The cement is poured down the chute into the hole.

The driver of this truck collects and delivers money. The truck is made of very strong metal. It has special locks to stop thieves from stealing the money.

This truck carries all the equipment needed to broadcast a television program. It can travel anywhere to show events as they happen.

Big Trucks

The longest trucks are made of two parts joined together. The cab where the driver sits is hooked onto a loaded trailer. The connection that joins the two parts swivels. This makes it easier for the driver to turn the truck around tight corners.

Can you see the forklift loading up the trailer?

Some trucks can pull two trailers! This cab is towing two trailers loaded with huge boxes. How many wheels can you see?

The truck's engine is under the cab. The driver tilts the cab forward so he can check the engine.

# Driving a Truck

Truck drivers often travel hundreds of miles to deliver their loads. The cabs have to be comfortable. They have big windows that give a good view of the road. What can you see in this driver's mirror?

On long journeys, the driver parks the truck and sleeps in an area behind the cab. There is even a TV set!

Carrying Cars

Most cars are built to drive on the road, but sometimes cars need to be carried by trucks. These new cars are being taken from the factory on a car transporter. How many cars can this transporter carry?

A racing car can only be driven on a race track. It is taken to the track in a truck like this. The platform rises up and the car is pushed inside.

Sometimes trucks break down. This special truck can carry other trucks to a garage to be repaired.

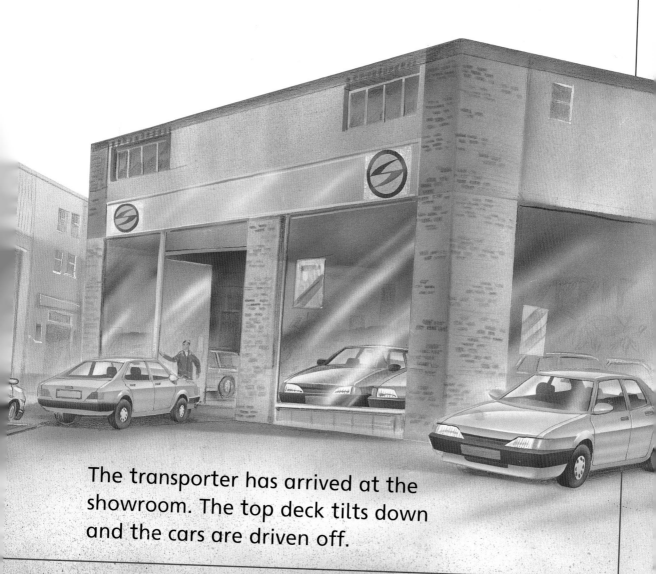

The transporter has arrived at the showroom. The top deck tilts down and the cars are driven off.

Tankers

Some tankers carry liquids, such as gasoline or milk. Large walls inside the tanker stop the liquid from swilling about. Gasoline is being unloaded from this tanker into storage tanks below the gas pumps.

This tank is raised up so that the load inside the tanker can be poured out. The other tanker is ready to be emptied.

Tankers also carry sugar and flour. The flour inside this tanker is kept very dry.

Cleaning Up

Different trucks keep streets clean and collect garbage. Garbage cans are tipped into the back of the green truck. A big plate pulls the garbage into the truck. What are the workers near the orange truck doing?

This street cleaner has brushes to sweep the street. The long hose is used to suck up fallen leaves and litter.

16

The Ramrodder is a truck that clears blocked drains by sucking up the garbage. Here it is at work in the streets of New York in the United States.

The garbage is squashed flat against another plate inside the garbage truck.

More garbage can now be crammed in. Can you see the worker using the controls?

Extra Big Loads

Sometimes extra big or very heavy loads have to be moved from one place to another. In Australia, trailers are linked together to make road-trains. They often travel across the desert at night because it is too hot during the day.

These heavy pieces of machinery need several long trailers to carry them.

This truck is the biggest in the world. It is carrying a space shuttle to the launch site. It moves on huge tracks instead of wheels. Can you see them?

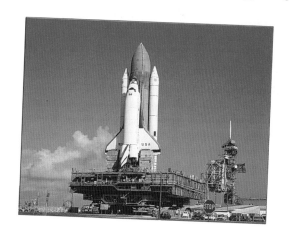

Snow Clearing

Snow trucks clear the roads of snow. A snow blower works fast. It churns up the snow and blows it off the road. Can you see the chains wrapped round the tires? The chains help to stop the truck from slipping on icy roads.

A snow plow has a huge blade on the front. The blade shovels the snow to the side of the road.

This truck follows behind the snow blower and spreads grit. The grit will make the road less slippery.

Off-road Trucks

Some trucks are not allowed to drive on the road. These huge dump trucks are carrying heavy rocks from one part of a quarry to another. The back tips up and the rocks slide off. The wheels of the truck are bigger than the driver!

This truck travels along a rocky road to take food to people who need help.

Racing trucks power round a race track. Drivers need special skills to race these powerful trucks.

Glossary

Broadcast	To send out.
Chute	A slide or trough.
Desert	Bare area of land. Most deserts are very hot.
Forklift truck	Truck with a platform at the front for lifting.
Grit	Small pieces of stone and sand used on icy roads.
Poisonous	Dangerous to eat or breathe.
Quarry	Place where rocks are dug out of the ground.
Ready-mixed	Something that is ready to use.
Refuse	Garbage.
Shovel	To push.
Showroom	Place where people can look at cars before buying them.
Space shuttle	Resuable spacecraft launched by rockets that returns to Earth like an airplane.
Swivel	To turn round.
Transporter	Large truck that carries heavy goods, like cars.

Index

More Books To Read

Koons, James. *Monster Trucks*. Mankato, Minn.: Capstone, 1996.
Koons, James. *Pickup Trucks*. Mankato, Minn.: Capstone, 1996.
McNaught, Harry. *Truck Book*. New York: Random House, 1978.
Schleifer, Jay. *Big Rigs*. Mankato, Minn.: Capstone, 1996.